Isaac Edwards Clarke

An Oration Delivered at the River House

Washington Heights - on the fourth of July, 1867

Isaac Edwards Clarke

An Oration Delivered at the River House
Washington Heights - on the fourth of July, 1867

ISBN/EAN: 9783337392048

Printed in Europe, USA, Canada, Australia, Japan

Cover: Foto ©Andreas Hilbeck / pixelio.de

More available books at **www.hansebooks.com**

An Oration

DELIVERED AT

The River House,

WASHINGTON HEIGHTS,

On the Fourth of July, 1867,

BY

Col. I. Edwards Clarke.

BOSTON:
PRESS OF GEO. C. RAND & AVERY, NO. 3, CORNHILL.
1867.

TO

THE GUESTS OF THE RIVER HOUSE,

THIS ADDRESS,

DELIVERED AND PUBLISHED AT THEIR REQUEST,

IS

RESPECTFULLY DEDICATED.

INTRODUCTION.

THE guests of the RIVER HOUSE, having resolved to celebrate the 4th of July, 1867, requested R. D. LIVINGSTON,
Esq., to read the Declaration of Independence, and Col. I. ED-
WARDS CLARKE to deliver an oration; while Messrs. CAMP and
WADE, with the assistance of the ladies, were to provide a
concord of sweet sounds, and give, for the inspiration and
delight of the guests, the national songs.

A temporary stage, draped with flags, was erected upon the
piazza; and at 11, A.M., the audience was called to order by D. M.
PORTER, Esq., who presided. Shaded from the sun, and fanned
by the sea-breeze sweeping up the river, the broad piazza made a
model auditorium; and few audiences on that day could have
been more pleasantly accommodated.

"America" was first sung, then the Declaration was admirably
read by Mr. LIVINGSTON, followed by the singing of "The Star
Spangled Banner;" then came the address, after which the choir
gave "The Red, White, and Blue." After thanks, by resolution, to
the reader and orator, the address was requested for publication.
The audience were then taken charge of by SAMUEL A. WALSH,
Esq., and his efficient assistants, Messrs. F. J. WEEKS and H. G.

HERRICK, a veteran of the Virginia campaigns, whose attentions enlivened the festivities, and were gratefully appreciated. At 2, P.M., Mr. HERRICK invited the guests to a sumptuous dinner, worthy the day, and the high reputation of the RIVER HOUSE. Under the shade of the grove, in the afternoon, the gentlemen whiled away the hours; and it seemed unanimously conceded that all had enjoyed themselves, and that the celebration was a success.

To the guests of the RIVER HOUSE, for 1867, as a reminiscence of pleasant mutual acquaintance and of happy hours, this memento is offered by the Committee.

ORATION.

IT has been thought fitting, that upon this day, when over the broad continent thirty millions of people rest from labor in order to celebrate the natal day of this great Republic, that we, who find ourselves grouped under this friendly roof, should join in the grand chorus of joy, which, beginning in the far-off forests of Maine, hailed the earliest rays of the morning sun, and, sweeping gradually westward, as half the world revolves, will greet the setting sun from the golden gate of the Pacific and the silvery shores of Sitka!

Gathered from so many homes, we find ourselves, for these summer months, thrown into association as one family: it were passing strange if on all topics we held harmonious opinions; but to-day, surely, spite of diverse associations or party "shibboleths," — to-day we have a common interest, a common sympathy; for we are, above all else, Americans!

Our great orator, when he would give a vivid impression of England's sway, pictured, in his unequalled diction, " Her morning drum-beat echoing round the world." Magnificent as is the imagery, and comprehensive as is the sway, it is, after all, but the drum-beat of a hireling soldiery, standing sentinel over distant and scattered colonies, and, in suggestiveness and sublimity, falls immeasurably below the spontaneous outburst of this peopled continent, which the sun of this day wakes and witnesses, " from the rising even to the going down thereof."

This morning, in the farthest village of Maine, when the sun's first ray flashed from the gilded vane of the church-spire, it woke the merry peals below; smiting sudden music from the tower, as of old, flashing along the Lybian sands, it was wont to wake the statued god to music. Instantly, as with some rare species of morning glory, the bare pole set in the village green blossomed into the flag; while, at the first sound of the bells, came the answering boom of joyful cannon! So, from hamlet to hamlet, the glad news speeds: hills and mountains catch up and fling back from their reverberating cliffs the joyous echoes. The White Hills of New Hampshire echo it to the Green

9

Mountains; the Green Mountains call across to the Catskills; these shout along the line to the Alleghanies, who, gathering up and multiplying the echoes among their multitudinous hills, send it far across the continent to the mighty ranges of the Rocky Mountains, which repeat the strain, till, as the fading sunlight gilds their topmost peak, old ocean learns the story, and seems, with his breaking billows along the shore, to murmur it as a lullaby to the sleeping continent!

There is no wilderness so desolate, no little hamlet so remote, no wanderer so forgetful, as not to heed and welcome this glad day.

The anniversary of that day which ushered into the august company of sovereign states a new republic, destined to a mightier sway than any imperial or regal dominion; the birthday of a nation, — ay, more, far more, — the beginning of an era to man; an era whose early steps it is in our power to trace, and from whose morning splendors we can prophecy the brightness of its perfect day; an era, not of the growth and prosperity of one nation only, but of progress to all mankind; an era which shall culminate when the vision of the poet is realized, —

"When the war-drum throbs no longer, and the battle-flags are
        furled,
In the parliament of man, the federation of the world."

2

We are standing upon historic ground,—on the
banks of this lordly river, whose very name per-
petuates the romance of its discovery, and whose
history is linked with the most tragic event of the
Revolution. This stream, in itself and its history,
furnishes an epitome of our country, our growth,
our destiny. Flowing, with stately sweep, between
mountains whose grandeur more than matches "the
castled crags that guard the Rhine," by meadows
fair as those that line the Thames, and beside
gentle acclivities, whose villa-crowned beauty recalls
those low hills that cluster around the flowered city
of Arno's stream; at last, under yonder frowning
Palisades, it passes out to meet the ocean, through
a gateway as magnificent as that of any stream that
seeks the sea. In its varied beauty and grandeur,
its inexhaustible resources, and its untamable might,
it may fitly symbolize this fair land, over whose
broad domain Nature has lavished her wealth of
power and beauty with no niggard hand; nor can
we forget that its waves once upheld that little
craft, whose rapidly-turning wheels prophesied and
made possible those sailless fleets whose keels have
since vexed every sea. Across to yonder valley
paddled, in his light canoe, the hero-chief of Coop-
er's romance; a little above us, Irving made classic
forever long reaches of river and shore; beside

this very spot slowly sailed, in the evening twilight, that British man-of-war which carried André and brought back Arnold! Every spot around us has been trodden by Redcoat and Tory and Continental, in those dark days when the infant republic struggled on to an uncertain end. You may trace mound and rampart and bastion still, and imagination re-peoples these woods and rocks with the struggling combatants.

A son of genius, born beside this stream, peopled its Highlands with fairies in that most exquisite poem, " The Culprit Fay," and, in another moment of inspiration, penned those matchless lines to his country's flag, which will live as long as poetry charms, or patriotism inspires.

Turning from the memories that cluster around the banks of this beautiful river to the present, we find in it a true index of our country's mighty growth. Who, passing a day of luxurious idleness upon this broad piazza, could fail to be impressed with the wonderful vitality, resources, and wealth of this country?

The crowded steamers that throng its waters; the fleets of barges, with their guardian tugs, moving in unending procession; the sails, that fly to and fro all the day; and, ever and anon, the thundering trains, flashing by, — swift shuttles, weaving the nation's cloth of gold. All things show that a mighty people are paying tribute to some imperial city.

Standing, then, where the memories of the Revolution still linger, and where the population and the production of the nation passes, as it were, in review before us, it seems peculiarly fitting that we, to whom past and present thus appeal, should pause for a moment, to remember what it is that this day commemorates, and to consider what, in view of the future of our country, is our duty as patriots and as citizens.

The teaching of history has been compared to the stern lights of the ship, illuminating only the path that has been passed, but shedding no radiance to pierce the palpable darkness of the future; but, to one who believes in a Divine Providence, that watches over the destinies of nations as of individuals, there is a solemn fascination in tracing,. while reading history, the unerring logic of events; to see Nemesis ever standing by the side of states; to mark how the present is the child of *all* the past; and how the future inevitably springs from the present. Philosophy and Science are fast demonstrating that there *is* no "chance,"— that order is Heaven's first and latest law. Buckle and Agassiz, wittingly or unwittingly, show Philosophy

and Science, standing, as of old, the willing hand-
maids of Religion; and the thoughtful student of
history is forced to exclaim with the poet, —

" Yet I doubt not through the ages one increasing purpose runs,
And the thoughts of men are widened with the process of the
suns."

Recall for a moment the discovery of this country, the long delay of colonizing it, the almost
miraculous preservation of the feeble and scattered
colonies, the recovery of the continent from the
Latin and Catholic powers, the gradual steps that
led to the concentration and final independence
of the sometime separate and unfriendly colonies;
review the subsequent events down to the present
moment, and doubt, if you can, the overruling
guidance of a Divine Providence.

In the light of the Emancipation Proclamation,
the inscription upon that bell whose mellow music
first rang out the thrilling news of the signing of
the Declaration was *not* a mere coincidence. Not
exultation only, but warning, mingled with its
tones, had they been heard aright, " Proclaim LIB-
ERTY throughout the land, to ALL the inhabitants
thereof."

It was in the same year that the " Mayflower"
landed at Plymouth that the first slave-ship touched

at Jamestown. For two hundred and forty years the two systems introduced by these two ships developed themselves over the fresh and boundless territories of this unsettled new world. Contrast Massachusetts and Virginia to-day, and see the logical results of the two civilizations. Recall the horrors of the past seven years, count up the untold millions wasted in war, and see whether slavery (but for which secession had not been) *is*, on the whole, "profitable."

Surely, though

> "The mills of God grind slowly,
> Yet they grind exceeding small."

I doubt, if, to every human being who has toiled in slavery, fair wages had been paid through all those two hundred and forty years, the sum-total would have amounted to more than was destroyed by the devastation of the war, paid to the soldiers, and burned up in ammunition.

Leaving the present, let us strive, for a moment, to realize the state of affairs as they were in 1776. Ninety-one years ago to-day, a few men, assembled in Philadelphia as Delegates of "the United American States, in Congress assembled," solemnly published and declared to the world the reasons that induced these thirteen colonies to throw off their allegiance to the king of England, and to declare themselves free and independent States. In terse, pregnant sentences, they recited the wrongs which had been endured by them until endurance was no longer possible; and solemnly commending their cause to the care of the God of nations, and to the judgment of the civilized world, they calmly awaited the issue. It was a sublime exhibition of courage.

Three millions of people, — less by one-fourth than the present population of this State of New York, — scattered over an extent of country reaching from New Hampshire to Georgia; with not a single town of importance which was not a seaport, and liable to sudden destruction by an enemy whose boast it was to rule the seas; without arms, without money, without preparation, — calmly inviting destruction.

The trials, the sufferings, the endurance, the patient, persistent courage displayed for seven long years, all culminating in that final triumph which made the celebration of this day possible and obligatory, — are they not familiar as household words?

> "The land is holy where they fought,
> And holy where they fell;
> For by their blood that land was bought, —
> The land they loved so well."

Usually the founders of new States and the authors of new creeds seem unconscious of their high destiny.

> "The hand that raised St. Peter's dome,
> And groined the aisles of Christian Rome,
> Wrought in a sad sincerity;
> Himself from God he could not free;
> He builded better than he knew:
> The conscious stone to beauty grew."

But, among those immortal signers of the Declaration, there was one on whom the spirit of prophecy seemed that day to rest, as he wrote to his wife, at Quincy, the story of that summer day's work, and stated that "it will be celebrated by succeeding generations as the great anniversary festival; commemorated, as the day of deliverance, by solemn acts of devotion to God Almighty; solemnized with pomp and parade, with shows, games, sports, guns, bells, bonfires, and illuminations, from one end of this continent to the other, from this time forward forevermore."

Among those who are recalled this day, the prophet, John Adams, should surely be honored; for never did prophet prophecy more truly.

So many years of peace had made the story of war obsolete; so great discoveries and triumphs in the physical world had hidden the work of the fathers, just as the carved and glistening marble hides the solid granite foundations below. So imperative was the demand for work, in development, by railroads, of this vast and ever-extending territory, that, to many, a day given up to the history of old battles, and encomiums upon the American Eagle, seemed a day wasted, and a fit subject of ridicule.

But, fortunately, the American people would not give up their *only* holiday. They would continue to march in processions, and sit long hours while some village orator told over again the stories of the Revolution; and in the little red schoolhouses scattered all over the New-England hills, and the far-away Western prairies, the children learned the story of Lexington and Bunker Hill. They might know nothing of the world's great battles; of Marathon or Thermopylæ, of Agincourt or Waterloo: but they *did* know of Valley Forge and Trenton and Yorktown. Fighting for country against the British was all the history we had; and the stupidest urchin of them all, though he might fail to comprehend the mysteries of "the three r's,—reading, 'riting, and 'rithmetic,"—did learn to hate the Britishers, to love the Continentals, to despise the Tories, and to worship Washington. And so it was, when the need came, the children of the Revolutionary sires justified their descent.

3

The astute conspirators, who thought the time had come to execute their long-planned treason, left out of calculation the Fourth-of-July orations, the little red schoolhouses, and "The Child's History." They should have remembered, that, as the Tories went down before the wrath of the old Continentals, so would their children, the Northern allies of secession, sink into insignificance before the awakened wrath of the descendants of Revolutionary sires.

They should have remembered, moreover, that it was not the recital of wrongs endured which gave to that Declaration its vital force; it was not the simple, indignant uprising against unendurable oppression, which gave to our Revolutionary fathers that success which justifies the Declaration, and redeemed rebellion from the stigma of treason. It was because that Declaration contained a seminal principle, because it announced the absolute political equality of the individual man, because it was the first translation of the Golden Rule into human politics, because it was a "Bill of Rights" for humanity, the "Magna Charta" of the whole human race; that, like the cloud by day, and the pillar of fire by night, it led those struggling patriots safely through the Red Sea and the wilderness.

It is that living principle, which sheds around those words, and the memory of those who first uttered them, the fragrance of immortality.

When the originators of secession put forth THEIR Declaration of Independence, mistaking the letter for the spirit, they enumerated, in justification of rebellion, a long list of supposititious wrongs endured; but they forgot that it was the vitalizing spirit of freedom which gave life and victory to their great original. When they invoked the inspiration of slavery, they surely forgot the words of that Thomas Jefferson who wrote the Declaration of '76, as, speaking of slavery, he said, " I tremble for my country when I remember that God is just."

They forgot the countless procession of dusky forms, which, for nearly two and a half centuries, had been passing through the portals of death; going out from poverty, from slavery, from torture, to plead for JUSTICE against their oppressors, before Him " whose arm is not shortened that it cannot save."

Their doom was fixed by inexorable fate. Had it not been so from the first, what cause could have succeeded when burdened with the atrocious crimes of Andersonville? But no sacrifice, no heroism (and of these there was no lack), could save their cause. "The stars in their courses fought against Sisera;" and theirs was a "lost cause" ere ever the wind of the bay had borne away the smoke-clouds from Sumter on that portentous April day. The champions of secession were as the bad man in Massinger's play, when he says, —

"My arm is weighted down with widows' prayers,
And my sword glued to its scabbard with wronged orphans'
    tears."

How the youthful hosts of freedom rallied at their country's call!

" Freedom's flag above them waving, freedom's songs, triumph-
    ant sung ;
Ne'er, I ween, to such an army, foe the gauge of battle flung."

Above and around their undisciplined ranks hovered, as we may be permitted to conceive, those shining hosts seen by the servant of the prophet, when, at his master's prayer, his eyes were opened before the walls of Dothan.

Not wholly an idle imagination was it that saw the avenging ghost of old John Brown, ever marching in the van, and marshalling the armies of the Republic; for it is not true, as the too desponding poet sang,

"That Truth is forever on the scaffold, Wrong forever on the
    throne."

No: sometimes it is permitted to mortal eyes to behold the grand earthly coronation of Justice, so that Faith may not wholly fail. But at what a price it triumphs! Number the desolated homes and hearts all over our Northern land. From what countless battle-fields, from what suffering beds of hospitals, from what inconceivable horrors at Belle Isle and Andersonville, the pale heroes of the loyal nation took up their line of march to join the armies of the skies! How the joyful ranks of the shining hosts opened to receive them! We may picture Warren welcoming Ellsworth, and be sure that the thousands, pressing on steadily after him, were each joyfully received by some kindred spirit of that countless army of martyrs who have died for the cause of human progress.

But these mourning Northern homes, thus desolated, are not all homes of hopeless sorrow. Many a father, bringing back the body of his brave son "to rest amid familiar scenes," has been ready to exclaim, with Cato, —

"Thanks to the gods! My boy has done his duty!
Welcome my son! There sit him down, my friends,
Full in my sight, that I may view at leisure
The bloody corpse, and count those glorious wounds.
How beautiful is death when earned by virtue!
Who would not be that youth? What pity 'tis

That we can die but once to save our country!
Why sits that sadness on your brow, my friends?
I should have blushed if Cato's house had stood
Secure, and flourished in a civil war!

Mourn not, then, overmuch for the loyal dead: —

"On Fame's eternal camping-ground
Their silent tents are spread ;
And Glory guards, with solemn round,
The bivouac of the dead."

Of the countless dead who died fighting for the alien flag, doubtless thousands were inspired by honest convictions of duty: of each of these we can but say, —

"No farther seek his merits to disclose,
Or draw his frailties from their dread abode, —
(There they alike in trembling hope repose), —
The bosom of his Father and his God."

A touching incident was told me by one who fought bravely in the Southern ranks. A fellow-officer, of whom he uttered a noble eulogy, fell in his arms on the rampart of Fort Wagner, whispering, with his latest breath, "My only regret in dying is, that I die fighting on the wrong side."

"The wrong side!" In the belief that this is the unspoken conviction of thousands, I largely base my hope of future unity and harmony.

We have now glanced rapidly at the cause, and stated the reasons, that have justified the universal celebration of the fourth day of July. Its future is assured. History, as if fearful, that, among these later brilliant deeds, some day more fortunate might usurp its place, took care to write against the date Vicksburg, Port Hudson, and Gettysburg.

The colonial period of our country never really closed till the war of secession began. We still looked to the mother-country for decisive words in law and literature. Suddenly, we have become, by virtue of military strength, a power among the nations. As surely as the great oak lies folded in the acorn's cup, so surely was our present free America contained in those opening sentences of the Declaration. Never had mighty drama more fitting prologue. Ours has been a natural development. The death-struggle between liberty and slavery was inevitable. It rests with us, now, whether those fiercely-contested victories of the war shall stand justified upon the book of fate; or whether they shall shine upon the pages of our country's history *only* as the vain heroism of that wild charge at Balaklava, which illumined the murky fight with a courageous splendor worthy the old chivalric days, but which, in no wise, aided to decide the contest, — brilliant but inconclusive, — a very meteor of battle.

We stand now at the very meeting of the ways: we may take, as we elect, the path that leads to republican freedom or centralized despotism. Rarely, in the history of a nation, is it thus given to a single generation to shape its destiny. We have seen how our woes arose from causes in the control of the men who shaped the new-born State: let us seek to spare our children similar suffering. Let us bury the bitterness of war. Let its hatreds and animosities be bygones. While, in the lately rebellious States, we must, in common prudence, keep the power in loyal hands till assured that the rights of all will be secured; as soon as possible, let the country be re-united.

In this new country of ours, the noble principles of the Declaration have become vital facts; and the political equality of man, without regard to color, race, or creed, has been embodied in the Constitution, and enacted in the law. At last, the experiment, whether a government "of the people, by the people, and for the people," is possible, is to be fairly tried. The civilization and Christianity of a people, is to be measured, not by the condition of the highest, but of the humblest. There is no foundation upon which a nation can build, save that of equal and exact Justice.

Our republican institutions have passed through

a fiery ordeal,—such an ordeal as no other system of government has ever successfully endured. They are yet upon trial. It is the solemn duty of every citizen to give now his best, most earnest thought to his country. Revolutions go not backward. The *status quo ante bellum* never *quite* returns. A broader, better civilization opens before us, or the loss of all we sought in the republic threatens. These are *not* idle fears. Where men claim the rights, they should not shrink from the duties, of sovereigns. It is yet to be demonstrated whether we have virtue enough to rescue and preserve, in all their pristine purity, the principles of republican government. Let us look, for a moment, at our dangers. Four millions of people forcibly changed from slaves to freemen; ten States, devastated by war, and, since the hurricane of war has subsided, starved by the failure of crops, are now under military rule; taxes over the whole land, more onerous than those of any other civilized country; an army of tithe-collectors, organized upon a system needlessly oppressive and inquisitive; a mixed foreign population, necessarily ignorant of the duties and dangers of republican citizens.

Whether, by the long-continued attrition of an inquisitorial revenue regime, the character of our people will not be essentially changed or modified,

4

is a grave question. Whether the habit of unquestioning obedience to official commands, engendered by military discipline, and patiently endured during the war; and whether the old Federalist leaven of desire for centralization, destructive to all republican freedom; the known tendency of every department of government to aggregate power to itself; and the long exercise of unprecedented power by every department,—are compatible with that individual independence which is the most essential element in the character of an American citizen, or whether all these new and exceptional influences are more than counterbalanced by our training before the war, are questions for thoughtful consideration.

The apparent dangers to arise from the sudden disbanding of enormous armies were shown to be *but* "apparent." When a million of soldiers sank back into the people, — as the rain drops into the ocean, — the citizen soldiery of the Republic, the bronzed veterans of a hundred battles, became but simple citizens; and the chimera of a military despotism, subverting our form of government, disappeared. High-spirited, independent, impatient of impertinent interference, acknowledging no superior, submitting to no unjust authority, giving to all the political rights claimed for each; obeying the law, because creating it, and therefore able to change it if found obnoxious; tolerant of religious opinion, because believing it a question between the Creator and the individual; respectful to rulers, because they were the executors of the law, while vigilantly watchful that they should be faithful servants of the people; intelligent, and careful that common-school education should be universal; industrious, capable, honest, patriotic, — such should be, in theory, the character of a citizen of a republic, such the product of its principles; and such was, in fact, the character of the free-born American citizen. When that character shall have become essentially changed, republicanism, as we have understood it, will become impossible. The necessity, imposed by the war, of a minute, all-embracing system of taxation, is the most dangerous change our revolution has thus far produced. This tendency must be balanced by careful education, and by the constantly instilled idea that *this* system, as well as the creation of military governments over the Southern States, is *but* a temporary expedient, rendered necessary by the misfortunes of war; and while it is to be endured, as offering the only honorable solution of our difficulties, it is not, in itself, to be commended or long continued.

We have now fully considered the depressing

conditions that surround our country, and can profitably note the encouraging features that should give cheerfulness and hope. Strong in the passionate love and devotion of her sons, our beloved and victorious Country calmly awaits the future. Burdened, as we are, with the enormous debt contracted to save the Republic, our burdens are not as great, in view of our rapidly-augmenting resources, as were those which rested upon our fathers at the close of their seven-years' war. To their three millions of population, we oppose thirty millions; for their narrow strip of Atlantic sea-coast, we have half a continent; and the mighty Mississippi is now

" A nation's heart, whose hands,
Far to eastward, far to westward, touch the shining
ocean sands."

We measure distance by thousands of miles; but steam and lightning so dominate space, that *our* extremest limits are *nearer* than were theirs. With them, population grew by slow accretion; to us, the thronging thousands escaping from Europe turn the ocean to a ferry. Invention has so multiplied the capability of the laborer, that now one man accomplishes the labor of four in those days. Over all the land, Providence again smiles with the promise of a bounteous harvest, and Peace stands waiting to shelter us under her white wings. Southern cotton-fields and Northern prairies welcome the returning laborers. He who lately toiled under the musket, now "jocund drives the plough a-field." Labor, armed with pick and spade, delves among precious metals in the mountain mines. Commerce marshals her fleets to bring to us the products of the Far East. All things prognosticate an era of material development, which shall make the burden of our national debt, a few years hence, so light as to be no longer burdensome.

Nearly four centuries ago, the bold Genoese set sail from Palos, seeking India, and found the New World. For four hundred years, men have spoken of the happy chance by which, when in pursuit of a delusion, he found immortal fame. But, lo! within the past eight months, we have demonstrated his theory, proving that, though dying in ignorance of the fact, he had nevertheless found what he sought, — the shortest way to the Indies. In the world's history, the control of the commerce of the East has ever signified wealth and dominion. Its possession has been the most eagerly-coveted prize between nations. To-day, beyond a peradventure, that commerce is ours. Into our coffers, "Ormus and Ind," China, and Far Japan, shall pour "barbaric gold." Draining Europe of population, and Asia of wealth, America shall stand the centre and con- troller of the earth. All lands shall acknowledge her might, and pay tribute to her power.

Within the lifetime of some who now hear me, a hundred stars shall cluster on that banner, and a hundred millions of happy people gather beneath its folds.

The Latin races in the New World have utterly failed; only the Anglo-Saxon, with his Irish and German cousins, prospers. Whether, as free citi- zens, either the African or Asiatic can be con- joined, is still a problem.

Down to the border-line of Mexico, a common language, common origin, common traditions, and common interests, point to a common government. The physical configuration of the continent implies unity of ownership; for the dwellers by streams that drain a continent will never submit to seek the sea through alien lands.

> " Our Union is river, lake, ocean, and sky :
> Man breaks not the medal when God cuts the die."

We may condemn the acquisition of territory, and shrink from foreign immigration : it is but fight- ing against fate. As well seek to dam the Mis- sissippi, or forbid the Atlantic waves to beat against our shores.

It is often said that the principles of republican-ism will fail when applied to large territories. Why? The principles of local self-government in local matters, to which, as speedily as possible, we must return; the idea that that government is best which governs least, rigidly applied to the General Government; no taxation without representation; no union of Church and State; no privileged classes; perfect equality of all citizens in civil and political rights; universal elementary education, enforced, if need be; strict subordination of the military to the civil power, as soon as congressional representations and local State Governments are fully restored to the States lately in rebellion, — what reason exists, in the nature of things, now that the strange anomaly of slavery has been annihilated, why *these* principles should not apply to a hundred States as well as to thirteen or thirty? Republican institutions are *not* a failure. The wisdom of the Fathers *is* justified.

At the close of the last century, after success gave emphasis to the words of the Declaration, its echoes were heard in Europe. Everywhere the people stepped up on to a wider field. Now that republican institutions here come forth so trium-phantly from trial, a far grander effect in Europe may be looked for. Already, it seems as if some new drama were about to be exhibited on the stage of the world's history. The closing of an old era, the opening of a new, is upon us. Old civilizations and future promise stand forth for all men to see. Wonderful mediæval pageants, recalling the past magnificence of emperor and pope, have just been displayed at Pesth and Rome; while at Paris, all the mightiest rulers of the earth have assembled to look upon the products of earth's workers. The kings pay homage to the people, to the toiling millions, and recognize the royalty of labor. When the people shall universally comprehend this, *their* reign begins.

Among us, some men are so wedded to past *forms* as to be unable to see aught but danger in any change, regardless of its cause or obvious necessity, and would hamper the new nation with the old traditions; but life mocks at dead forms, and the vitality of our country, which so terrifies them, is its sure hope. At the Navy Yard at Charlestown, they will take you into an immense ship-house, and there show you a vessel upon the stocks, where it has stood for years. The work of preparing her for sea was long since abandoned; but there she stands, an object of interest to idle gazers, an excellent thing by which to learn how a ship looks when half-built, but, for all the practical purposes of a ship, as utterly useless, as if the noble trees, that gave their lives to contribute the massive timbers that form her keel and shapely ribs, were still waving, in all their leafy splendor, along the slopes of rock-ribbed Katahdin. They have lost the life of the tree, and utterly missed the grander life of the ship. What idea of a ship would one have who should never see any ship but that? How utterly would the true idea of the ship, — the full-rigged ship, spreading every sail, like some mighty bird poised over the water, an image of triumphant power, of all-conquering beauty, or scudding with bare poles before the angry waves, like a hunted deer, — fail of entering his imagination!

The " Ship of State " has furnished metaphor alike to poet and orator; but I have thought, ofttimes, that it was the long-housed ship on the stocks, and not the real child of the sea, after which they modelled. To ride out the storms of turbulent populations, to bear the passengers *safe* over the trackless sea; that is the end and object of the ship: therefore it is to the practical sailing qualities, not *simply* to the "constitutional" ribs, that the eyes and thoughts of the statesmen, the navigators, must be directed. How to keep the ship true to her course, how to avoid the rocks and reefs and lee-shores of politics, these are the problems. I know no other guides than the fixed stars of principle. They must know well the heavenly landmarks who would navigate safely over unknown seas. When clouds and tempest obscure the stars, sad will it be for that nation whose pilots have not some compass by which to lay the line true to the pole. For republican statesmen, that compass is to be found alone in an innate, unalterable love of Liberty and Justice. Such pilots has the good Ship found in times past, nor, under God's guidance, shall she lack them in the days to come.

www.ingramcontent.com/pod-product-compliance
Lightning Source LLC
Chambersburg PA
CBHW030915260626
47169CB00008B/2858